THE ONE CUSTOMER CEO

TRANSFORMING BUSINESS THROUGH RELENTLESS CUSTOMER FOCUS

SIDHISHWARR

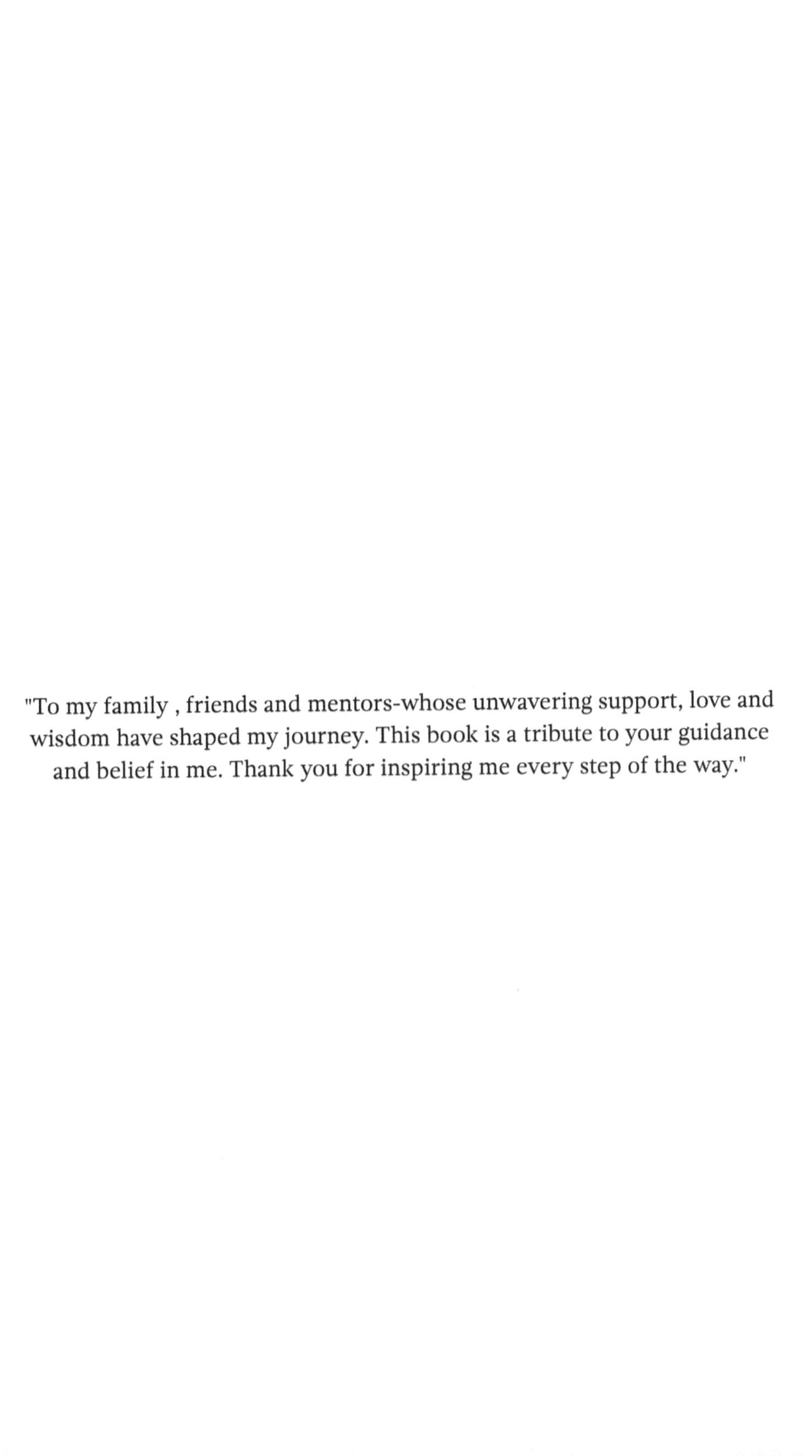

"To my family , friends and mentors-whose unwavering support, love and wisdom have shaped my journey. This book is a tribute to your guidance and belief in me. Thank you for inspiring me every step of the way."

Contents

Foreword

When I was first introduced to the concept of "The One Customer CEO," it struck a chord deep within me. In my career spanning decades in the Food manufacturing and supplier to Major Food Brands in QSR industry and retail industry. I've witnessed firsthand how businesses rise and fall not just because of their products or operations, but because of how well—or poorly—they connect with their customers.

The QSR industry, in particular, is a battlefield for customer loyalty. You aren't just competing on price or taste; you're competing for the hearts and minds of people who can choose from dozens of other brands at any moment. I've always believed that the secret to success lies in one powerful principle: the customer is not just a stakeholder in your business; the customer is your business.

What this book does so brilliantly is articulate a framework that transforms this principle into a way of life for future CEOs and leaders. It challenges the traditional notion of leadership, one that often prioritizes profits, processes, or internal benchmarks. Instead, it makes the case for a customer-first approach that doesn't just drive financial success but builds something far greater—a legacy of trust, loyalty, and impact.

I've had the privilege of working with Leader that embraced this philosophy. At times, it required hard decisions, like investing in customer research when budgets were tight, revisiting operational processes to enhance the customer journey, or personally getting involved to resolve customer complaints that seemed small at first glance but had the potential to shape long-term perceptions. Each of these decisions wasn't always easy, but they always paid off.

The beauty of The One Customer CEO lies in its simplicity. It focuses on one customer at a time. This resonates deeply with me because too often, businesses fall into the trap of treating customers as numbers, segments, or categories. They forget that behind every data point is a real person with emotions, expectations, and choices. By putting the spotlight back on that one customer, this book reminds us that the path to business excellence isn't paved with spreadsheets but with meaningful, human connections.

I'm also deeply moved by the practical insights this book offers. It goes beyond theory and gives leaders actionable tools to embed customer-centricity into every layer of their organizations. From mapping the customer journey to redefining success metrics like Net Promoter Scores (NPS) and Customer Lifetime Value (CLV), the book equips leaders with strategies that are both visionary and grounded.

One of the most critical lessons I've learned as a leader is that customer-centricity isn't the responsibility of one department—it's the DNA of the entire organization. Whether it's your frontline team delivering exceptional service, your supply chain ensuring timely delivery, or your marketing team crafting messages that resonate, every function plays a role in delighting the customer. This book beautifully captures that essence, illustrating how customer obsession can unite teams, dissolve silos, and create a culture of excellence.

I also want to highlight the courage it takes to lead with a customer-first mindset. There will be challenges—resistance from internal teams, external market pressures, and the ever-evolving expectations of customers. But as this book shows, the rewards far outweigh the risks. The stories of leaders who embraced this philosophy, the practical templates for implementation, and the clear, actionable guidance make this book an invaluable resource for CEOs at any stage of their journey.

To any CEO, aspiring leader, or business professional reading this foreword: this book isn't just a guide; it's a mindset shift. It's an invitation to rethink how you lead, how you measure success, and how you connect with the people who make your business possible.

I am honored to write this foreword because I know firsthand the transformative power of the ideas within these pages. By becoming a The One Customer CEO, you're not just building a successful business—you're creating something that people trust, admire, and return to time and time again.

As you embark on this journey, remember: it's not about the millions of customers you aim to serve—it's about how you serve that one customer in front of you right now. Everything else will follow.

— AASHVINII RINDHE
Industry Leader and Advocate for Customer-Centric Leadership

Preface

In a world where businesses are constantly competing for growth, innovation, and market dominance, the one thing that often gets lost in the chaos is the customer. Despite all the advancements in technology, strategy, and operations, many organizations still fall into the trap of focusing on profits and efficiency at the expense of those who sustain them— their customers.

This book, The One Customer CEO, is a call to action for leaders to rethink their priorities, redefine success, and realign their businesses around a single, unwavering focus: the customer.

The premise is simple yet transformative: to build extraordinary businesses, you must start with one satisfied customer at a time. By focusing on individual customers—truly understanding their needs, desires, and pain points—you not only create exceptional experiences but also cultivate loyalty, trust, and long-term growth.

As a CEO or leader, you are uniquely positioned to set the tone for this transformation. Your actions, decisions, and priorities have the power to ripple through your organization, inspiring teams, delighting customers, and disrupting industries. But to achieve this, you must first embrace a new mindset—one that puts the customer at the heart of every decision and recognizes that their success is inseparable from your own.

Throughout this book, we'll explore what it takes to become a "The One Customer CEO." You'll learn how to:

- Transition from a profit-first to a customer-first leadership approach.

- Build a culture of customer obsession that permeates every department.

- Measure success using customer-centric metrics like Net Promoter Score (NPS), Customer Lifetime Value (CLV), and more.

- Innovate by listening to and involving customers in the process.

- Overcome the inevitable challenges of embedding customer-centricity into your organization.

You'll find real-world examples, actionable strategies, and tools to help you along the way. From the inspiring stories of leaders who've revolutionized their industries by prioritizing the customer to practical templates for mapping customer journeys, this book is designed to equip you with everything you need to lead with purpose and impact.

This isn't just a business book—it's a leadership manifesto for the modern era. Whether you're running a startup, scaling a mid-sized company, or steering a multinational corporation, the principles in this book are universal. They apply to any business in any industry because, at the end of the day, customers are the common denominator of all success.

In writing this book, I drew inspiration from years of observing and working alongside extraordinary leaders who understood the power of focusing on one customer at a time. Leaders like Bhupinder Singh, whose customer-first approach helped customer and organization into a beloved brand BEHIND BRAND. And countless others who proved that when you listen, empathize, and deliver, customers don't just buy your product—they become your advocates, your partners, and your most valuable assets.

As you read, I invite you to think about your customers. Not as abstract data points or sales figures but as people with real needs, challenges, and aspirations. Imagine what your business could achieve if every decision was made with their success in mind.

This book is about more than just creating great customer experiences—it's about leaving a legacy. The legacy of a leader who cared, listened, and acted. A leader who didn't just aim for quarterly profits but built a business that customers loved, employees were proud of, and competitors envied.

Welcome to the journey of becoming a "The One Customer CEO". It's a path of purpose, resilience, and incredible rewards—not just for your business but for the customers who make it all possible.

Let's get started.

Acknowledgements

Writing *The One Customer CEO* has been a journey of deep exploration into what truly drivescustomer centric leadership. This book would not have been possible without the support, insights and encouragement of many individuals.

First and foremost, I extend my heartfelt gratitude to Mr. Bhupinder Singh for his invaluable guidance and belief in this vision. His wisdom and perspective helped shape the core principles of this book.

A special thanks to my family for their unwavering patience and understanding, and encouragement throughout this process. Your support has been my greatest strength.

To my colleagues, industry experts and thought leaders who shared their experiences and perspectives- your insights have been instrumental in making this book rich in real world relevance.

I also want to express my appreciation to Notion Press team for their support, expertise and dedication in bringing this book to life with clarity and impact.

Lastly to my readers- leaders, entrepreneurs and professionals striving to create exceptional customer experiences- this book is for you. I hope it serves as guide to transforming the way businesses engage with their most valuable asset *The One Customer.*

Thank you all

Prologue

Organizations are constantly striving for growth, efficiency, and innovation. Yet amid the relentless pursuit of success, one crucial element often gets overlooked-the customer. The truly exceptional companies, the ones that stand the test of time recognize that their greatest asset isn't their product, technology, or strategy, but rather the deep and unwavering focus on one fundamental entity The Customer.

The book, *The One Customer CEO,* is a journey into the mindset and strategies of leaders who have mastered the art of customer-centric leadership. It is not just about delivering great service or creating an outstanding product- it is about reshaping the very foundation of how business operate, from boardroom decisions to frontline interactions.

Through real-world examples, insightful frameworks, and actionable strategies, this book will challenge conventional thinking and inspire business leaders to reimagine their role-not just as CEOs, executives, or entrepreneurs, but as One Customer Officer. It will guide you in building an organization where every decision, investment, and innovation revolves around delivering unparalleled value to the One Customer-The one who define your success.

As you turn the pages, prepare for transformative journey that will not only reshape your approach to leadership but also redefine the way your business thrives in an ever-evolving market. Because in the end, the true measure of success is not just growth, but the enduring trust and loyalty of the one customer who matters most.

Welcome to *The One Customer CEO*

CHAPTER I

The New Role of the CEO

In today's business arena, the role of the Chief Executive Officer (CEO) is undergoing a seismic shift. Traditionally, CEOs were perceived as the guardians of profitability, the stewards of financial growth, and the architects of operational efficiency. While these responsibilities remain critical, a new paradigm is emerging: the customer-first CEO. This chapter explores the journey from a profit-first mindset to a customer-centric leadership approach, examining how this shift reshapes company culture and creates long-lasting value.

Transitioning from Profit-First to Customer-First Leadership

The historical role of CEOs as profit-first leaders was born from an era when shareholders were the primary stakeholders. The sole mission was to maximize returns, often at the expense of employees, customers, and even long-term sustainability. This singular focus on profit drove strategies that prioritized cost-cutting, operational scale, and rapid market expansion. However, the tides have turned.

In the age of hyper-connectivity and instant feedback, customers have become more than just end-users of products; they are active participants in shaping a brand's narrative. CEOs can no longer afford to view customers as transactional entities. Instead, the most successful leaders recognize that putting customers at the center of decision-making not only drives loyalty but also fuels sustainable growth.

Why the Shift is Imperative

The Power of Choice: In a globalized economy, customers are empowered with countless alternatives. A single misstep—poor service, lack of transparency, or ignoring feedback—can drive them to competitors. CEOs who embrace customer-first leadership acknowledge that retaining customer trust and loyalty is more valuable than chasing short-term gains.

The Digital Age of Accountability: Social media and review platforms have made companies accountable to their customers in unprecedented ways. A poor customer experience no longer stays confined; it goes viral. CEOs who adopt a customer-first mindset proactively address issues, mitigating risks to reputation and fostering goodwill.

The Link Between Customer Experience and Profitability: Contrary to popular belief, a customer-centric approach doesn't sacrifice profitability. Studies show that companies prioritizing customer experience achieve higher retention rates, increased word-of-mouth referrals, and even command premium pricing. A satisfied customer is a repeat customer—and a brand advocate.

Building a Customer-First Culture: The CEO's Role

The transformation to a customer-centric organization starts at the top. A CEO's vision sets the tone for how a company approaches its customers. But transitioning to this mindset requires more than just verbal commitment; it demands actionable steps that ripple across every level of the organization.

- **Redefining Success Metrics:** Profit margins and shareholder returns can no longer be the sole metrics of success. Customer satisfaction, Net Promoter Scores (NPS), and lifetime customer value must take equal precedence. For example, Jeff Bezos famously adopted a customer-first mentality at Amazon by focusing on "delighting the customer" even when it meant lower short-term profits.
- Empowering Teams: CEOs must foster a culture where every employee, regardless of their role, feels a sense of ownership toward the customer experience. This can be achieved by decentralizing decision-making, providing customer service training, and tying incentives to customer satisfaction rather than just financial outcomes.
- Listening to the Frontlines: The frontline employees—those interacting directly with customers—often have the most valuable insights. A customer-first CEO makes it a point to listen to these employees, incorporating their feedback into strategic decisions. For example, Howard Schultz of Starbucks regularly held meetings with baristas to understand customer needs and innovate accordingly.
- Leading by Example: A CEO's actions resonate louder than words. When a CEO takes a personal interest in resolving customer issues or participates in customer feedback sessions, it sets a powerful example for the rest of the organization.

The Ripple Effect of CEO-Driven Customer Focus

When a CEO embraces a customer-first philosophy, it creates a ripple effect that transforms the entire company culture.

- Enhanced Employee Engagement: Employees are more motivated when they see the direct impact of their work on customers. A customer-first culture fosters a sense of purpose, aligning employee efforts with a greater mission. For instance, Zappos' customer-centric ethos, championed by its late CEO Tony Hsieh, led to higher employee satisfaction and retention rates.
- Stronger Cross-Functional Collaboration: A customer-first approach breaks down silos. Departments like marketing, sales, operations, and customer service must work together to deliver seamless experiences. This collaboration often leads to innovation and efficiency.
- Brand Loyalty and Advocacy: When a company's culture revolves around customer satisfaction, it translates into consistent, high-quality customer experiences. This builds trust, turning customers into loyal advocates. Apple's legendary customer loyalty is a testament to this principle.
- Resilience in Adversity: A customer-centric organization is better equipped to weather crises. When customers trust a brand, they are more forgiving during rough patches. For example, during the COVID-19 pandemic, companies like Airbnb and Zoom retained customer loyalty by prioritizing customer needs over immediate profits.

Practical Steps for CEOs to Embark on the Journey

- Audit the Customer Journey: Start by identifying pain points in the customer journey. CEOs should personally experience their company's products and services, gaining firsthand insight into what works and what doesn't.
- Establish Open Communication Channels: Make it easy for customers to share feedback, whether through surveys, focus groups, or social media platforms. Use this data to inform strategic decisions.
- Invest in Technology: Leverage tools like customer relationship management (CRM) systems, data analytics, and artificial intelligence to understand customer behaviour and predict future needs.
- Create a Feedback Loop: Ensure customer feedback reaches all levels of the organization, from the C-suite to the frontlines. Celebrate successes and address failures transparently.
- Be Prepared for Pushback: Transitioning to a customer-first model may initially face resistance, especially if the organization is deeply

entrenched in a profit-first mindset. CEOs must remain steadfast, communicating the long-term benefits of this approach.

The Transformational Potential of a Customer-First CEO

The customer-first CEO is not just a leader; they are a visionary who recognizes that business is fundamentally about relationships. By putting customers at the heart of decision-making, CEOs can achieve a level of impact that transcends financial success.

Consider Satya Nadella of Microsoft, who transformed the company's culture by focusing on customer needs and empathy. Under his leadership, Microsoft not only regained its competitive edge but also became a customer-driven innovation powerhouse.

Similarly, Indra Nooyi's tenure at PepsiCo demonstrated how aligning business goals with customer satisfaction and social responsibility can drive both profitability and brand reputation.

The transition from profit-first to customer-first leadership is not just a trend—it is a necessity in a world where customers hold unprecedented power. CEOs who embrace this change will not only future-proof their organizations but also leave a legacy of trust, loyalty, and enduring success.

As we delve deeper into this book, we will explore actionable strategies, case studies, and frameworks to help CEOs lead with a customer-first mindset, transforming their companies into thriving, customer-centric organizations. The journey begins here—with a commitment to put the customer first, always.

Customer-centricity is not just a buzzword; it is the foundation of sustained business success. A robust customer philosophy focuses on understanding, satisfying, and exceeding customer expectations. This philosophy integrates empathy, proactive solutions, and mutual trust into every customer interaction.

This book explores the pillars of customer philosophy, formulates actionable steps, and provides examples to illustrate its real-world application.

The Formula for Customer Satisfaction (CS): The FIVE Framework

To create a successful customer philosophy, we begin with a simple formula:

Where:

- CS = Customer Satisfaction

- E = Experience (Positive interactions across all touchpoints)
- V = Value (Perceived worth of product/service)
- I = Innovation (Solving new or existing customer problems creatively)
- F = Friction (Any barriers in the customer journey)

Example:
Amazon's commitment to reducing friction (e.g., through one-click purchasing and fast delivery) enhances both experience and perceived value. This results in high customer satisfaction, evident in its customer loyalty metrics.

Pillars of a Customer Philosophy

a. Empathy: Understand the Customer

Empathy is the foundation of any customer-centric approach. It involves seeing the world through the customer's lens.

How to implement empathy:

- Use tools like persona mapping to understand different customer types.
- Train employees in active listening and emotional intelligence.

Example:
Starbucks' teams are trained to personalize drinks and engage in meaningful conversations, fostering emotional connections with customers.

b. Value Creation: More Than Just Products

Customers seek value beyond the tangible product or service. This includes emotional, social, and functional value.

- Benefits include quality, customer service, and brand experience.
- Costs include monetary expense, time, and effort.

Example:
Apple's premium pricing is justified by its ecosystem of high-quality products, sleek design, and seamless integration, creating a high perceived value.

c. Trust Building: Consistency and Transparency

Trust is built when businesses deliver on their promises consistently and are transparent about their processes.

Strategies to build trust:

- Honesty in marketing and advertising.
- Consistent delivery of promises, such as on-time shipping.
- Proactively addressing mistakes with accountability.

Example:

Zappos, an online retailer, built trust by offering a no-questions-asked return policy, showing confidence in their products and care for customers.

d. Proactive Solutions: Solving Problems Before They Arise

Anticipating customer needs and solving problems before they occur ensures a seamless experience.

How to achieve this:

- Use predictive analytics to foresee customer pain points.
- Implement feedback loops to improve continually.

Example:

Netflix's recommendation engine uses customer data to suggest personalized content, reducing decision fatigue and enhancing satisfaction.

Building a Customer-Centric Culture

A philosophy is only as strong as the culture that supports it. To embed customer-centricity into your organization, follow the C.A.R.E. framework:

C.A.R.E. Framework

- Communicate: Share the importance of customer focus with employees.
- Align: Align business goals with customer needs.
- Recognize: Reward employees who excel in customer service.
- Evaluate: Continuously assess and refine customer strategies.

Example:

Southwest Airlines empowers employees to make decisions that benefit customers, such as waiving fees or rebooking flights, aligning with its customer-first philosophy.

The Future of Customer Philosophy

A forward-thinking customer philosophy evolves with changing trends and technologies. As businesses navigate the digital age, customer expectations will continue to rise. Companies that embrace innovation, empathy, and proactive strategies will lead the way.

"The One Customer CEO" my experience with Bhupinder Singh of Vista Processed Foods Pvt. Ltd.

In the world of business leadership, the term "The One Customer CEO" refers to a leader who prioritizes customer-centricity above all else, aligning the company's vision, strategy, and operations to serve a singular purpose: exceeding customer expectations. Such a CEO considers every business decision, whether operational or strategic, through the lens of the customer's needs and satisfaction. Bhupinder Singh, the Managing Director and CEO of Vista Processed Foods Pvt. Ltd., exemplifies this concept, demonstrating how putting customers at the core of a business strategy can lead to exceptional success.

My definition of a "The One Customer CEO"

The essence of being a "The One Customer CEO" lies in embedding customer satisfaction into the DNA of an organization. This involves not only addressing immediate customer needs but also anticipating future expectations. A One Customer CEO exhibits the different customer centric characteristic

- His Customer-First Vision: The CEO aligns the company's mission and vision with customer-centric goals. He viewed the business as a solution to the customer's problem.
- His Empathy and Engagement initiatives : A One Customer CEO started building a culture of empathy, ensuring that all employees understand and value the customer's perspective.
- His Data-Driven Decision-Making: Customer insights, derived from data and feedback, formed the foundation of all strategic decisions.
- His Commitment to Quality and Innovation: He always focussed on delivering consistent value and embracing innovation to meet evolving customer demands, no matter what the situation was.
- His Responsiveness and Accountability: His leadership maintained open lines of communication with customers, taking accountability for mistakes and learning from feedback.

Bhupinder Singh: The One Customer CEO in Action

Being a freshly recruited directly from college Person to a Lead in Food Safety and Quality Assurance function I have seen the first CEO as Bhupinder Singh who dliligently trained people in his entire career through allowing them to make mistakes, coaching and mentoring. He encouraged teams to discuss errors and mistakes so that systems can be built further by putting people first in such situations.

As the CEO, Bhupinder Singh has championed a customer-first philosophy, ensuring that Vista's operations are fine-tuned to meet the stringent quality standards and preferences of its customers. His leadership reflects a deep understanding of what it means to be a "The One Customer CEO."

He practices and demonstrated a Customer-First Philosophy throughout his interaction and even now as I am writing this chapter he is still thinking how we can do better.

For Mr. Bhupinder Singh, the "one customer" is not a specific individual but a representation of every stakeholder who interacts with the brand — from multinational food chains to end consumers enjoying the final product. Mr. Singh's approach ensures that the Company remains not just a supplier but a trusted partner for its customers.

One of the most notable examples of Bhupinder Singh's customer-centricity is Vista's long-standing partnership with a customers in India by supplying frozen and fresh products and through relentlessly working towards adhering to strict global standards of quality, hygiene, and safety.

Key Customer-Centric Initiatives:

- He ensured that Company adapted its product offerings to meet Customer specific requirements, such as customised solutions the processes and requirements of customers
- He implemented rigorous quality control and assurance measures to meet global standards. Singh understood that consistent quality was non-negotiable for the customer.
- He fostered the culture of transparency as fostering transparent communication channels, Company earned customer trust, which translated into a long-term partnership.

This commitment to quality and customer satisfaction allowed to expand its scope, becoming a critical supplier for many customers in India.

Another hallmark of his leadership is Company's focus on innovation driven by customer needs. He recognized early on that customer preferences in India are highly dynamic and regional. To cater to this diversity, he focussed on investing heavily in research and development to Support customer.

- Recognising that global customers value sustainability, He led initiatives to reduce Vista's carbon footprint by optimizing manufacturing processes and manufacturing location This not only aligned with customer values but also enhanced Company's "Brand behind brand" reputation.

The 4 Cs of CEO

His success as a "One Customer CEO" can be attributed to his implementation of the following framework, which he calls the 4 Cs of Customer-Centric Leadership:

- Collaboration: He believes that strong collaboration between an organization and its customers is key to success. He has worked tirelessly to establish partnerships based on mutual trust and shared goals. Collaborating with its customers during the product development phase, ensuring that the final output aligns perfectly with customer expectations.
- Consistency: for him , consistency in product quality and delivery timelines is non-negotiable. He ensures that every batch produced at Vista meets stringent global standards. To maintain consistency, he implemented advanced manufacturing practices like HACCP (Hazard Analysis Critical Control Points) and Food Safety certifications across all production facilities.
- Communication: He emphasizes the importance of regular and transparent communication with customers. This ensures that customers are aware of every step in the production and delivery process. During the COVID-19 pandemic, He proactively communicated with its customers about potential supply chain disruptions and offered solutions to mitigate the impact.
- Commitment: His unwavering commitment to customer satisfaction is evident in his willingness to go above and beyond to meet customer demands. When Customer introduced its new global initiative for healthier food, he ensured that Company aligned its products with these new nutritional standards, showcasing his adaptability and customer-first mindset.

What the Impact of Customer-Centric Recognising?

Under his leadership, Company has built enduring relationships with its customers. The trust and loyalty of global brands are testaments to his customer-focused approach. The Company has experienced exponential growth, with its revenues and market share increasing year over year. This growth is directly tied to Singh's ability to prioritize customer satisfaction and innovate accordingly.

The Organization is now recognized as a leader in the frozen food processing industry, with several awards for quality and innovation. This reputation stems from his customer-centric leadership.

What I learnt from Mr. Bhupinder Singh while his way of "Becoming a One Customer CEO"

He always focussed on Anticipating Customer Needs: Just as Mr. Singh adapted Company's offerings to Indian tastes and global standards, CEOs must constantly innovate to meet evolving customer preferences.

He Said Embedding Quality in the Culture is very important.

His emphasis on consistency in quality underscores the importance of integrating quality assurance into every business process.

The One Customer CEO Values Collaboration

Building long-term partnerships, as Singh did with Major customer base requires transparency, mutual trust, and shared goals.

Adapt while Innovating

His commitment to sustainability and product innovation highlights the need to align business strategies with customer values and trends

His leadership at epitomizes the concept of a "The One Customer CEO". His relentless focus on quality, innovation, and customer satisfaction has not only propelled Organization to the forefront of the food processing industry but also set a benchmark for customer-centric leadership. Prioritizing the needs of his "one customer" — whether it's Customer or the end consumer — he has demonstrated how businesses can achieve lasting success through empathy, collaboration, and a commitment to excellence.

Aspiring leaders can draw valuable lessons from Mr. Singh's journey, understanding that the path to sustainable growth and industry leadership lies in putting the customer first, every single time.

CHAPTER II

Know Thy Customer

In business, the age-old mantra "know thy customer" has never been more critical than it is today. Understanding your customer isn't just a matter of knowing their demographic profile; it's about diving deeper into their needs, desires, behaviors, and pain points. This chapter explores how to develop a deep connection with your customers, the tools available to gather meaningful insights, and the strategies to build a comprehensive view of your "One Customer."

The Importance of Knowing Your Embedding

In the past, businesses relied on assumptions about customers, often lumping them into broad categories. However, the modern customer expects personalization, authenticity, and relevance. Companies that fail to understand their customers risk losing them to competitors who are willing to invest the time and resources to truly connect.

Why It Matters:

- Customer Retention: Understanding your customers helps you anticipate their needs and provide solutions before they look elsewhere.
- Brand Loyalty: Customers are more likely to stick with brands that "get" them and reflect their values.
- Innovation: Deep insights into customer pain points drive the creation of better products and services.
- Profitability: Happy customers become repeat customers, and their loyalty often leads to higher lifetime value.

To truly know your customer, businesses must go beyond surface-level information and create a robust understanding of the individual behind the transaction.

How to Truly Understand Your Customers

Identify Their Needs

Customers choose products and services to solve specific problems or fulfill desires. Identifying their needs involves uncovering both functional and emotional motivators.

- Functional Needs: These are the practical problems customers are trying to solve. For example, a busy professional might need a food delivery service to save time.
- Emotional Needs: These are tied to how customers want to feel. For instance, they might choose a sustainable brand because it aligns with their values, making them feel responsible and empowered.

Map Their Pain Points

Understanding customer pain points is key to building trust and loyalty. Pain points can arise in various stages of the customer journey:

- Awareness: Customers struggle to find the information they need.
- Consideration: Confusion about pricing, features, or benefits prevents them from making a decision.
- Purchase: Complex checkout processes or unexpected costs lead to frustration.
- Post-Purchase: Lack of support or follow-up leaves them dissatisfied.

Addressing these pain points, companies can create smoother, more enjoyable customer experiences.

Understand Their Desires

Customers' desires often go beyond solving problems—they want experiences that delight them. These desires might include:

- Customization and personalization.
- A seamless, frictionless experience.
- A brand that aligns with their values and lifestyle.

Practical Tools for Gathering Customer Insights

To truly understand customers, businesses must actively gather and analyze data. Here are some of the most effective tools for gaining insights:

Surveys: Surveys remain one of the most direct methods of collecting customer feedback.

- Customer Satisfaction Surveys (CSAT): Measure customer happiness with a product, service, or interaction.
- Net Promoter Score (NPS): Gauge the likelihood of customers recommending your brand.

- Market Research Surveys: Identify broader trends in customer behavior.

Best Practices:

- Keep surveys concise and focused.
- Use a mix of quantitative (e.g., ratings) and qualitative (e.g., open-ended questions) formats.
- Incentivize participation with discounts or other rewards.

Feedback Loops: Establishing feedback loops ensures that customer insights are continually gathered, analyzed, and acted upon.

- Transactional Feedback: Ask for input immediately after a purchase or interaction.
- Periodic Feedback: Conduct regular check-ins to understand changing needs and preferences.
- Two-Way Communication: Encourage dialogue through support channels, social media, and community forums.

Social Listening: Social listening involves monitoring online conversations about your brand, industry, or competitors to uncover insights.

- What to Look For: Mentions of your brand, customer complaints, reviews, and emerging trends.
- Tools to Use: Platforms like Sprout Social, Brandwatch, or Hootsuite.

Social listening not only helps understand customer sentiment but also allows companies to proactively address issues and engage with their audience.

Data Analytics: Data analytics tools can help create detailed profiles of customer behavior.

- Web Analytics: Understand how customers navigate your website.
- Purchase History: Identify buying patterns and preferences.
- Customer Relationship Management (CRM): Build a comprehensive view of each customer.

Examples:

- Amazon uses analytics to recommend products based on past purchases.
- Spotify provides personalized playlists based on listening habits.

Building a 360-Degree View of Your "One Customer"

The concept of the "One Customer" involves consolidating all available information into a single, holistic view of an individual customer. This approach helps businesses deliver personalized, seamless experiences at every touchpoint.

Data Integration: To create a 360-degree view, integrate data from various sources:

- Purchase history.
- Social media interactions.
- Customer support tickets.
- Marketing campaign engagement.

Advanced CRM platforms like Salesforce or HubSpot can help centralize and organize this data.

Segmentation and Personalization: While building a complete profile is important, not all customers are the same. Segment your customer base into groups with similar behaviors or characteristics, and personalize your approach for each segment.

- A luxury retailer might focus on high-value customers with exclusive offers.
- A fitness app might send personalized workout plans based on user preferences.

The Role of AI and Machine Embedding: Artificial intelligence and machine learning can enhance customer understanding by identifying patterns and predicting future behavior.

- Chatbots: Provide instant, personalized support based on customer history.
- Predictive Analytics: Anticipate customer needs before they arise.

For example, Netflix uses AI to recommend shows and movies tailored to individual viewing habits, enhancing customer satisfaction and retention.

Turning Insights Into Action: Knowing your customer is only half the battle; the real challenge lies in using those insights to create meaningful experiences.

- Align Teams Around the Customer: Ensure all departments, from marketing to customer service, have access to the same customer insights and understand their role in delivering value.
- Adapt to Feedback: Use customer feedback to improve products, services, and processes. Demonstrate that you're listening by communicating changes back to the customer.

Measure Success: Track the impact of customer insights on key metrics like retention rates, customer lifetime value, and NPS.

The Bottom Line

Truly knowing your customer is not a one-time exercise—it's an ongoing commitment. By investing in the tools and strategies outlined in this chapter, businesses can build stronger relationships, foster loyalty, and drive long-term growth.

As the business landscape becomes increasingly customer-driven, the ability to deeply understand your audience will set you apart from competitors. When you know your customer at this level, you're not just meeting their expectations—you're exceeding them, time and time again.

CHAPTER III

The Customer–Centric Organization

In the modern business landscape, success hinges on one critical factor: the customer. A customer-centric organization is one where every decision, process, and interaction revolves around creating value for the customer. But customer focus isn't limited to a single department or team; it must permeate every aspect of the business—from sales and marketing to product development and operations.

This chapter delves into how organizations can embed customer focus into their DNA, empower employees to deliver exceptional experiences, and foster collaboration across departments to unify teams around a shared mission: delighting the customer.

Embedding Customer Focus into Every Department

To create a customer-centric organization, every department must understand how their work impacts the customer. This requires shifting perspectives and aligning goals with customer needs.

Sales: Building Relationships, Not Just Closing Deals

Traditionally, sales teams are evaluated based on how many deals they close. However, in a customer-centric organization, the focus shifts to building long-term relationships.

- Understanding Customer Pain Points: Sales teams must deeply understand the customer's challenges and offer tailored solutions.
- Consultative Selling: Rather than pushing products, salespeople act as advisors, helping customers find the best fit for their needs.
- Post-Sale Engagement: Sales doesn't end with a closed deal; it extends to ensuring customers achieve success with the product or service.

Marketing: Creating Value Beyond the Sale

Marketing is no longer just about promoting products—it's about creating value for the customer at every stage of their journey.

- Personalized Messaging: Use customer insights to craft messages that resonate with individual needs.

- Educational Content: Provide resources that help customers solve problems, even if they're not directly tied to your product.
- Customer Advocacy: Highlight success stories and turn satisfied customers into brand ambassadors.

Product: Designing with the Customer in Mind

In customer-centric organizations, product development begins and ends with the customer.

- Customer Input in Design: Involve customers early in the design process through focus groups, surveys, and beta testing.
- Iterative Improvement: Use customer feedback to refine and enhance products over time.
- Usability Over Features: Prioritize ease of use and real-world application over flashy but unnecessary features.

Operations: Ensuring Seamless Delivery

Operations may not interact directly with customers, but their impact is profound. A seamless customer experience depends on efficient, reliable operations.

- Streamlining Processes: Ensure that everything from order fulfillment to customer support is smooth and efficient.
- Proactive Problem-Solving: Anticipate potential issues and resolve them before they affect the customer.
- Sustainability: Today's customers care about the environmental and social impact of their purchases, so embedding sustainable practices into operations is key.

Empowering Employees to Deliver Exceptional Customer Experiences

A customer-centric organization empowers its employees to go above and beyond for customers. Empowerment involves giving employees the tools, training, and autonomy they need to make decisions that benefit the customer.

Training for Empathy and Excellence

- Customer Empathy Training: Help employees understand the customer's perspective and challenges.
- Continuous Learning: Provide ongoing training on product knowledge, communication skills, and problem-solving techniques.

Autonomy to Make Decisions

- Frontline Empowerment: Give customer-facing employees the authority to resolve issues on the spot without needing managerial approval.
- Encourage Initiative: Foster a culture where employees feel confident suggesting and implementing ideas that improve the customer experience.

Recognizing and Rewarding Efforts

- Celebrate Success Stories: Highlight instances where employees went above and beyond for customers.
- Incentivize Customer Focus: Align performance metrics and rewards with customer satisfaction rather than internal goals.

Companies like Zappos empower their customer service representatives to spend as much time as necessary with a customer to resolve their issue, creating memorable and positive experiences.

Breaking Down Silos to Unify Teams Around the Customer

One of the biggest challenges in creating a customer-centric organization is breaking down silos between departments. When teams work in isolation, they lose sight of the bigger picture and how their actions impact the customer.

Create Cross-Functional Teams

Bring together employees from different departments to work on customer-focused initiatives. This fosters collaboration and ensures a holistic approach to problem-solving.

A cross-functional team comprising sales, marketing, and product development might work together to improve the onboarding process for new customers.

Share Customer Data Across Teams

A unified view of the customer requires sharing data and insights across departments.

- Centralized CRM Systems: Use of tools like Salesforce or HubSpot to give all teams access to customer profiles and interactions.
- Collaborative Analytics Dashboards: Provide real-time visibility into customer behavior and feedback.

Align Goals and Metrics

Ensure all teams are working toward shared goals that prioritize the customer.

- Unified KPIs: Metrics like Net Promoter Score (NPS), customer retention, and lifetime value should be key performance indicators for all departments.
- Regular Alignment Meetings: Hold meetings where teams discuss progress toward customer-focused goals and share updates.

Leadership's Role in Breaking Embedding

Leadership must set the tone for collaboration by emphasizing the importance of customer focus in every decision and action.

- Lead by Example: Encourage leaders to work across departments and prioritize customer-centric initiatives.
- Communication from the Top: Regularly communicate the company's commitment to customer-centricity through town halls, newsletters, and other channels.

The Ripple Effect of a Customer-Centric Organization

When customer focus is embedded into the culture of an organization, the impact is felt far and wide:

- Happier Customers: A better understanding of customer needs leads to improved products, services, and experiences.
- Engaged Employees: Employees who see the positive impact of their work on customers are more motivated and fulfilled.
- Stronger Brand Reputation: Word-of-mouth from satisfied customers enhances brand perception and attracts new business.
- Increased Profitability: Loyal customers contribute to consistent revenue and lower acquisition costs.

Amazon is often hailed as a customer-centric organization. By embedding customer focus into every aspect of its operations—from personalized recommendations to hassle-free returns—Amazon has set a high standard for customer experience. This focus has not only driven customer loyalty but also positioned Amazon as a market leader.

A customer-centric organization doesn't happen by accident; it requires deliberate effort, cross-departmental collaboration, and a commitment from leadership. By embedding customer focus into every department, empowering employees, and breaking down silos, companies can create a culture where the customer is truly at the heart of everything they do.

CHAPTER IV

Designing the Ideal Customer Journey

In today's competitive market, delivering an exceptional customer experience is not just a differentiator—it's a necessity. The foundation of this lies in designing the ideal customer journey: a seamless, intuitive, and memorable path that aligns with the customer's needs, expectations, and emotions at every touchpoint. This chapter explores how to map the customer journey, identify key moments of delight and friction, and optimize internal processes to create a truly customer-centric experience.

The customer journey encompasses every interaction a customer has with your brand, from initial awareness to post-purchase support. Mapping this journey is the first step toward designing an ideal experience.

Step 1: Define the Stages of the Journey

A typical customer journey consists of the following stages:

- Awareness: The customer becomes aware of your brand or product.
- Consideration: They evaluate your offerings against competitors.
- Purchase: The transaction takes place.
- Onboarding: The customer begins using your product or service.
- Support: The customer seeks help or guidance post-purchase.
- Loyalty/Advocacy: A satisfied customer becomes a repeat buyer and brand advocate.

Step 2: Identify Key Touchpoints

Touchpoints are the specific interactions customers have with your brand at each stage. Examples include:

- Awareness: Social media ads, blog posts, influencer endorsements.
- Purchase: Website checkout, in-store experience, mobile app transactions.
- Support: Chatbots, customer service calls, FAQ pages.

Step 3: Understand Customer Expectations and Emotions

At each touchpoint, customers have specific expectations and emotions:

- Expectations: What customers want to achieve (e.g., quick support, easy checkout).
- Emotions: How they feel during the interaction (e.g., excitement, frustration).

- Customer Journey Mapping Formula

A simple formula for mapping each touchpoint is:
Touchpoint + Customer Expectation + Emotion → Opportunity for Optimization
Example:

- Touchpoint: Website checkout
- Customer Expectation: Fast and secure payment
- Emotion: Nervous about payment security
- Opportunity for Optimization: Add trust badges and offer multiple payment options.

Identifying Moments That Matter: Delight vs. Friction
Not all touchpoints are created equal. Some moments have a greater impact on the customer experience, either positively (delight) or negatively (friction).
Moments of Delight
Moments of delight occur when you exceed customer expectations, creating positive emotions and memories.
Examples:

- Personalized thank-you notes after a purchase.
- Surprising customers with free upgrades or gifts.

Moments of Friction
Moments of friction occur when customers encounter obstacles or frustrations in their journey.
Examples:

- Long wait times for customer support.
- Complicated return processes.

Delight vs. Friction Formula

To prioritize improvements, evaluate the impact of each moment using the following formula:

Impact = Frequency × Severity × Business Value

Where:

- Frequency: How often the moment occurs.
- Severity: How strongly it affects the customer's experience.
- Business Value: The potential gain or loss to the company (e.g., retention, revenue).

Aligning Internal Processes to Optimize the Customer Experience

A seamless customer journey depends on well-aligned internal processes. Every team and system must work together to deliver a consistent experience.

Step 1: Establish a Customer-Centric Culture

- Cross-Departmental Alignment: Encourage collaboration between marketing, sales, product, and support teams.
- Shared Metrics: Use customer-focused KPIs like Net Promoter Score (NPS) or Customer Satisfaction Score (CSAT).

Step 2: Leverage Technology

Technology can streamline processes and enhance the customer experience.

- CRM Tools: Centralize customer data to provide personalized experiences.
- Automation: Use chatbots, email automation, and AI for faster responses.
- Analytics: Monitor customer behavior to identify trends and areas for improvement.

Step 3: Design for Consistency

Ensure consistency across all touchpoints, both online and offline.

- Brand Guidelines: Use consistent messaging, tone, and design.

- Omnichannel Experience: Seamlessly connect channels like social media, websites, and physical stores.

Step 4: Test and Iterate

The ideal customer journey is never static. Continuously test, learn, and improve.

- A/B Testing: Experiment with different approaches to see what works best.
- Customer Feedback Loops: Regularly gather input and act on it.

Case Study: Designing a 360-Degree Customer Journey
Background:

A mid-sized e-commerce company wanted to improve its customer journey to boost retention and reduce churn.

Approach:

Mapping the Journey: The company identified key touchpoints, including website navigation, checkout, delivery, and support.

Moments of Delight and Friction:

- Delight: Surprise discounts during checkout.
- Friction: Confusing return policy.

Process Optimization:

- Introduced live chat for immediate support.
- Simplified the return process with prepaid labels.
- Used CRM software to personalize recommendations.

Results:

- Increase in customer satisfaction.
- Reduction in churn rate.
- Growth in repeat purchases.

Designing the ideal customer journey is an ongoing process that requires understanding your customers, identifying key moments, and aligning internal processes. By mapping the journey, addressing friction points, and enhancing moments of delight, companies can create a seamless and memorable experience that drives loyalty and advocacy.

CHAPTER V

Building Trust and Loyalty

In a world where customers have endless options, trust and loyalty are the cornerstones of long-term success. Customers today seek more than just products or services—they look for authentic relationships with brands that align with their values and deliver consistently. This chapter explores why trust is crucial, how to foster it through transparency and consistency, and strategies for turning satisfied customers into loyal brand advocates.

The Importance of Authenticity in Customer Relationships

Authenticity is the foundation of trust. Customers can easily detect insincerity or empty promises, and once trust is broken, it's incredibly hard to rebuild. Authenticity goes beyond marketing; it's about being genuine, honest, and true to your brand values.

Why Authenticity Matters

- Differentiation in a Crowded Market: Customers are more likely to choose brands that stand for something and resonate with their personal beliefs.
- Emotional Connection: Authentic brands create deeper, emotional bonds with customers.
- Resilience in Tough Times: Authentic relationships can weather challenges better, as customers are more forgiving of brands they trust.

How to Demonstrate Authenticity

- Define and Live Your Brand Values: Ensure your company values are clearly defined and embedded in your operations.

- Example: Patagonia emphasizes environmental sustainability, which is reflected in its products and marketing campaigns.
- Be Transparent: Share your successes and failures openly. Customers appreciate honesty over perfection.
- Engage Personally: Show your human side by interacting with customers authentically on social media, in emails, and during customer support interactions.

Key Insight:

- Authenticity is not about claiming to be perfect; it's about showing that you care and are constantly striving to improve.
- Strategies for Fostering Trust Through Transparency and Consistency
- Trust is built when customers can rely on a brand to deliver on its promises, every time. Transparency and consistency are critical for achieving this.

Transparency: Showing Customers What's Behind the Curtain
Customers today demand visibility into a company's operations, products, and decision-making processes. Transparency demonstrates that you have nothing to hide and fosters credibility.
Ways to Implement Transparency:

- Pricing: Be upfront about costs, including hidden fees or surcharges.
- Sourcing: Share where your products come from and how they are made.
- Sustainability: Highlight efforts to minimize environmental impact, such as carbon offsets or ethical sourcing.
- Customer Reviews: Display unfiltered reviews to show you value all feedback, not just the positive.

Case Study: Everlane

- Everlane, a fashion retailer, practices "radical transparency" by disclosing the true cost of producing their clothes, including materials, labor, and transportation. This approach has earned them a loyal customer base.
- Consistency: Delivering on Promises Every Time
- Consistency is about ensuring that every interaction a customer has with your brand meets or exceeds their expectations.

Steps to Ensure Consistency:

- Standardize Processes: Develop clear workflows for customer interactions, from purchase to support.
- Empower Employees: Train staff to uphold brand values and provide consistent service across all touchpoints.

- Quality Assurance: Regularly review products and services to maintain high standards.

Consistency Formula: Trust = (Promises Made × Promises Kept) ÷ Time

Insight:

The longer you consistently deliver on promises, the stronger the trust you'll build with customers.

Turning Satisfied Customers into Loyal Brand Advocates

Customer satisfaction is the first step toward loyalty, but true advocacy comes from going above and beyond to delight your customers. Brand advocates don't just return—they spread the word, bringing in new customers and reinforcing your reputation.

Exceeding Expectations

Delight your customers by surprising them in meaningful ways.

- Example: Sending a handwritten thank-you note after a purchase.
- Example: Offering a small freebie with repeat orders.

Creating Emotional Connections

People are more likely to advocate for brands they feel connected to emotionally.

- Storytelling: Share stories about your brand's mission, employees, or customers.
- Personalization: Use data to tailor experiences to individual customers, such as product recommendations or birthday discounts.

Encouraging Advocacy

Make it easy for satisfied customers to share their positive experiences.

- Referral Programs: Offer discounts or rewards for bringing in new customers.
- Social Media Engagement: Encourage customers to tag your brand in posts and feature their content.
- Testimonial Requests: Ask loyal customers for reviews or case studies that you can showcase on your website or marketing materials.

Key Metric: Net Promoter Score (NPS)

NPS measures how likely your customers are to recommend your brand to others. A high NPS indicates a strong base of advocates.

Practical Tools for Building Trust and Loyalty

CRM Software: Customer Relationship Management (CRM) tools help centralize customer data, making it easier to track interactions and personalize experiences.

- Example Tools: Salesforce, HubSpot, Zoho CRM.

Social Listening Tools

Monitor what customers are saying about your brand on social media to address concerns and identify advocates.

- Example Tools: Brandwatch, Hootsuite, Sprout Social.

Customer Feedback Platforms

Gather feedback to identify areas for improvement and build stronger relationships.

- Example Tools: SurveyMonkey, Qualtrics, Typeform.

Case Study: Starbucks' Loyalty Program

Starbucks is a masterclass in building customer loyalty. Their rewards program offers points for purchases, personalized offers, and free items on birthdays.

- Result: Increased customer retention and over 50% of U.S. sales from loyalty members.

What makes Starbucks stand out is not just the program itself but the emotional connection they've built. Customers feel valued and rewarded, making them more likely to advocate for the brand.

Building trust and loyalty requires more than great products or services—it demands authenticity, transparency, and consistency. By fostering meaningful relationships, exceeding expectations, and empowering customers to advocate for your brand, you can create a loyal customer base that drives growth and success.

CHAPTER VI

Innovation Through the Customer Lens

Innovation isn't about building something new—it's about creating solutions that truly resonate with your customers. The most successful innovations are those born from a deep understanding of customer needs, preferences, and pain points. In this chapter, we'll explore how to use customer feedback as a catalyst for innovation, the benefits of co-creating with customers, and how to strike a balance between responding to customer requests and staying aligned with your long-term strategic goals.

How to Use Customer Feedback to Drive Innovation

Customer feedback is one of the most valuable resources for any business aiming to innovate. When harnessed effectively, it can reveal hidden opportunities, highlight areas of improvement, and spark ideas for new products or services.

Listening to Your Customers

- Feedback Channels: Ensure customers can easily share their opinions. Use surveys, social media, online reviews, customer service interactions, and feedback forms.
- Social Listening: Monitor online conversations about your brand to understand unspoken needs or concerns.

Analyzing Feedback for Patterns
Innovation often begins with identifying recurring themes or challenges.

- Use AI Tools: Platforms like Qualtrics or Medallia can analyze large volumes of qualitative data to uncover trends.
- Categorize Feedback: Group feedback into categories such as usability, features, or customer service to spot patterns more easily.

Example:
Amazon's innovation of one-click ordering came directly from customer feedback about reducing friction during the checkout process.
Acting on Feedback

- Quick Wins: Implement small changes quickly to show customers their input is valued.
- Big Bets: Use feedback to inspire larger, long-term innovations, such as developing entirely new product lines.

Formula for Feedback-Driven Innovation:
Innovation = (Customer Needs + Organizational Capability) × Speed of Execution

The Role of Co-Creation: Involving Customers in Product Development
Co-creation is the process of actively involving customers in the development of products, services, or experiences. This approach not only results in better solutions but also fosters deeper customer loyalty.

Why Co-Creation Works

- Direct Insights: Customers provide real-world perspectives that internal teams might overlook.
- Stronger Buy-In: When customers feel they've contributed to a product, they're more likely to support and promote it.
- Reduced Risk: Testing ideas with customers early reduces the risk of developing unwanted products.

Methods for Co-Creation

- Focus Groups: Gather a small group of customers to provide feedback during the development process.
- Beta Testing: Allow select customers to test new products or features before launch.
- Innovation Workshops: Collaborate with customers in brainstorming sessions to solve specific challenges.
- Crowdsourcing: Platforms like Kickstarter or IdeaScale allow customers to contribute ideas or vote on concepts.

Examples of Co-Creation in Action

- Lego Ideas: Lego invites fans to submit designs for new sets, and the most popular ones are turned into official products.
- Nike By You: Nike's customization platform allows customers to design their own shoes, fostering creativity and personalization.

Balancing Customer Requests with Long-Term Strategic Vision

While customer feedback is invaluable, not every request should be acted upon. Some demands may align with short-term satisfaction but conflict with long-term goals. Striking the right balance is critical for sustainable growth.

Evaluating Customer Requests

- Alignment with Vision: Assess whether the request fits within your company's mission and values.
- Market Potential: Determine whether the idea appeals to a broad audience or a niche group.
- Feasibility: Evaluate whether the idea can be executed within your technical, financial, or operational capabilities.

Tool: Prioritization Matrix

Use a matrix to evaluate ideas based on impact and effort:

- High Impact, Low Effort: Implement quickly.
- High Impact, High Effort: Invest strategically.
- Low Impact, Low Effort: Address as time permits.
- Low Impact, High Effort: Deprioritize.

Avoiding the "Feature Creep" Trap

Adding too many features based on customer requests can dilute your product's core value.

- Example: Early smartphones focused on core features like calls and messaging. Adding too many apps initially would have overwhelmed users.

Innovating Beyond Immediate Demands

Great leaders anticipate needs customers don't yet realize they have.

- Steve Jobs' Philosophy: "People don't know what they want until you show it to them."
- Case Study: The iPod revolutionized music consumption by focusing on simplicity and integration with iTunes, a vision customers hadn't explicitly requested.

Aligning Innovation with the Customer Journey
Innovation is most impactful when it enhances the customer journey. Consider how new ideas will affect key touchpoints and eliminate friction.
Mapping Innovation to Touchpoints

- Pre-Purchase: Innovations like augmented reality (AR) for virtual try-ons enhance the decision-making process.
- Purchase: Seamless payment methods, such as digital wallets, simplify transactions.
- Post-Purchase: Robust customer support systems or loyalty programs ensure continued satisfaction.

Emotional Impact of Innovation

- Delight Moments: Create features or services that surprise and excite customers, like Apple's AirDrop for effortless file sharing.
- Reducing Friction: Eliminate pain points, such as streamlining account sign-ups with social media logins.

Practical Tools for Driving Innovation Through the Customer Lens
Design Thinking
This customer-centric approach involves empathizing with users, defining their problems, ideating solutions, prototyping, and testing.

- Tools for Design Thinking: Miro, Figma, Ideo's Field Guide.

Customer Journey Analytics
Analyze data from customer interactions to identify opportunities for innovation.

- Example Tools: Google Analytics, Mixpanel, Adobe Experience Cloud.

Innovation Labs
Create dedicated spaces for brainstorming and testing ideas with both employees and customers.
Tesla's Customer-Centric Innovation
Tesla's innovations are driven by customer insights:

- Pain Point: Customers worried about charging infrastructure.
- Solution: Tesla developed Supercharger stations, making EVs more practical.
- Pain Point: EVs were perceived as slow.
- Solution: Tesla introduced high-performance models like the Model S Plaid, redefining customer expectations.

Tesla's ability to listen to customers while staying ahead of the curve has made it a leader in the automotive industry.

Innovation through the customer lens is about more than meeting expectations—it's about anticipating needs, co-creating solutions, and enhancing the customer journey at every step. By leveraging feedback, involving customers in development, and balancing immediate demands with long-term vision, companies can create groundbreaking products and experiences that drive loyalty and growth.

CHAPTER VII

The Metrics That Matter

In today's customer-driven business landscape, financial metrics like revenue and profit are no longer the sole indicators of success. Companies must expand their focus to include metrics that capture the health of customer relationships and the value they bring over time. In this chapter, we'll explore key customer-centric metrics such as Customer Satisfaction (CSAT), Net Promoter Score (NPS), and Customer Lifetime Value (CLV). We'll also discuss how to measure, interpret, and act on customer feedback and align key performance indicators (KPIs) with a customer-first approach.

Moving Beyond Revenue: Metrics That Define Customer Success

Traditional financial metrics often overlook the factors driving sustainable growth—customer satisfaction, loyalty, and advocacy. Customer-centric metrics provide deeper insights into how your business meets customer needs and builds long-term relationships.

Customer Satisfaction (CSAT): CSAT measures how satisfied customers are with a specific interaction, product, or service.

Formula:

CSAT SCORE= (No. of Satisfied customer responses/Total number of Customer responses) x100

Example: After a customer service call, a survey asks, "How satisfied are you with the resolution?" Customers rate their satisfaction on a scale from 1 (very dissatisfied) to 5 (very satisfied).

Why It Matters:

- Reflects short-term customer happiness.
- Identifies pain points in specific touchpoints, such as onboarding or post-purchase support.

Actionable Insights:

- Low scores can pinpoint areas needing immediate improvement, such as customer support or product quality.

Net Promoter Score (NPS): NPS measures the likelihood of customers recommending your business to others. It's a strong indicator of loyalty and brand advocacy.

Question Asked:

"How likely are you to recommend our company to a friend or colleague?" (Rated from 0 to 10)

Formula:

NPS = (Promoters-Detractors)/Total Respondent x 100

Why It Matters:

- Strong correlation with customer loyalty and future growth.
- Helps identify brand advocates who can drive word-of-mouth marketing.

Actionable Insights:

- Engage with promoters to amplify their advocacy.
- Address concerns of detractors to reduce churn and improve experience.

Customer Lifetime Value (CLV): CLV estimates the total revenue a customer will generate over their entire relationship with your company.

Formula:

CLV = Customer Value x Average customer lifespan

CLV = (Average value of Sale) x (Average Number of Transactions) X (Average Customer lifespan)

CLV =Average revenue per user X Gross Margin/Churn Rate

Why It Matters:

- Highlights the long-term value of retaining customers versus acquiring new ones.
- Guides investments in customer retention strategies.

Actionable Insights:

- Use CLV to segment customers and tailor marketing efforts.
- Invest more in high-value customers who generate consistent revenue.

Customer Effort Score (CES): CES measures how much effort customers must exert to complete a task, such as resolving an issue or making a purchase.

Why It Matters:

- Simplifying processes reduces friction and increases satisfaction.
- Strong predictor of repeat business.

How to Measure and Act on Customer Feedback Effectively
Establishing Feedback Channels
Collect feedback through multiple channels:

- Post-Interaction Surveys: Triggered after customer service calls or purchases.
- Online Reviews: Monitor platforms like Google, Yelp, and Trustpilot.
- Social Listening: Analyze customer sentiments on social media platforms.

Analyzing Feedback
Feedback is only useful when it's analyzed effectively.

- Text Analytics: Use AI tools to analyze open-ended responses and identify common themes.
- Segmentation: Break down feedback by demographics, customer type, or touchpoints for actionable insights.

Closing the Loop
Once feedback is collected, act on it:

- Acknowledge: Thank customers for their input.
- Communicate Changes: Let customers know how their feedback is driving improvements.
- Measure Impact: Assess whether changes improve satisfaction, loyalty, or other key metrics.

Aligning KPIs to Reflect a Customer-First Approach
For a company to truly be customer-centric, its KPIs must align with customer-focused objectives.

Department-Specific KPIs

Embed customer metrics across all departments:

- Marketing: Track NPS, engagement rates, and conversion rates.
- Sales: Measure CLV and retention rates.
- Customer Service: Monitor CSAT, CES, and first-call resolution (FCR).
- Product Development: Track feature adoption rates and user satisfaction with new releases.

Balanced Scorecard Approach

A balanced scorecard includes both financial and non-financial metrics to create a holistic view of performance.

- Customer Perspective: How satisfied and loyal are our customers?
- Internal Processes: Are we optimizing processes to improve customer experiences?
- Innovation: Are we addressing customer needs through new products and services?

Using Real-Time Dashboards

Leverage tools like Tableau, Power BI, or Salesforce to create dashboards that provide real-time insights into customer metrics.

Real-World Example: Disney's Commitment to Customer Metrics

Disney tracks customer satisfaction at every stage of the guest journey:

- CSAT at Attractions: Surveys are collected immediately after guests leave rides.
- NPS for Resorts: Guests rate their likelihood of recommending Disney hotels to others.
- Operational Metrics: Metrics like average wait times and cleanliness scores are monitored daily.

Aligning these metrics with their overarching mission of delivering magical experiences, Disney ensures continuous improvement and customer loyalty.

The right metrics enable businesses to stay aligned with customer needs, track progress toward customer-first goals, and drive continuous improvement. Moving beyond revenue and profit metrics to focus on customer satisfaction, loyalty, and lifetime value creates a stronger foundation for sustainable growth.

39

CHAPTER VIII

The CEO as the Chief Listener

Leadership in the modern business world is no longer about standing atop the hierarchy and issuing directives. Instead, the most successful CEOs today understand the importance of stepping down from the tower to listen, engage, and act based on customer feedback. The One Customer CEO, a prominent figure in the Industry, exemplifies this philosophy. By prioritizing direct interaction with customers, he not only drives innovation but also strengthens the trust and loyalty essential to long-term success.

In this chapter, we'll explore why CEOs must take on the role of "Chief Listener," learn from real-world examples, and outline practical steps to stay connected to the lifeblood of any business: the customer.

Why CEOs Must Personally Engage with Customers

CEOs set the tone for the entire organization. When they prioritize listening to customers, it sends a powerful message throughout the company.

Driving a Customer-First Culture

A CEO's commitment to customer engagement inspires teams across departments to follow suit. Employees take cues from leadership, and a customer-centric CEO ensures that every level of the organization keeps the customer at the center of their work.

For instance, The One Customer CEO frequently emphasizes customer feedback in internal meetings with his teams. By encouraging product innovation based on real-world insights, he has fostered a culture where every employee—from marketing to operations—strives to meet customer needs.

Gaining Unfiltered Insights

Direct customer interactions allow CEOs to bypass the layers of filtered feedback that often distort the reality of customer experiences. Hearing unfiltered stories, pain points, and suggestions provides CEOs with actionable insights that drive meaningful change.

Building Customer Trust

When a CEO personally engages with customers, it humanizes the brand. It shows customers that their voices matter at the highest level, which builds trust and loyalty.

Success Stories: CEOs Who Made an Impact by Listening

Redefining Through Customer Engagement

In the fast-paced industry, the One Customer CEO exemplifies the power of listening. When a customer expressed dissatisfaction with the consistency of a popular product, The CEO didn't delegate the issue to lower management. Instead, he personally visited the restaurant, interacted with the customer, and worked with his product team to adjust the recipe. This hands-on approach not only resolved the issue but also led to an increase in customer satisfaction for that product.

By staying connected to customers, The CEO has driven innovation in menu offerings, streamlined operational processes, and even redesigned packaging based on customer preferences. His leadership demonstrates that customer engagement is not just a task but a strategic advantage.

Starbucks' Renaissance

When Howard Schultz returned as Starbucks' CEO in 2008, he embarked on a listening tour, visiting stores and talking to both employees and customers. By understanding their concerns, he implemented changes that revitalized the brand, including reintroducing the focus on high-quality coffee and customer experience.

Obsessing Over the Customer

Jeff Bezos, the founder of Amazon, famously leaves one empty chair in every meeting to represent the customer. This symbolic act reminds executives to always consider the customer's perspective when making decisions. Bezos has also been known to read customer complaint emails himself, ensuring he stays connected to Amazon's core audience.

Practical Steps for Staying Connected to Your Customers

Becoming the Chief Listener doesn't happen overnight. It requires intentional strategies and consistent effort.

Spend Time in the Field

CEOs must allocate time to visit stores, attend events, or participate in customer interactions directly.

- Example: Bhupinder Singh regularly visits QSR outlets during peak hours to observe operations, talk to customers, and gather insights.

Use Customer Feedback Tools

Leverage technology to stay connected to customer sentiment:

- Monitor NPS, CSAT, and online reviews personally.
- Engage on social media to respond directly to customer queries or complaints.

Establish Open Communication Channels
Create avenues for customers to share feedback directly with the CEO.

- Dedicated Email Address: Provide an email address (e.g., ceofeedback@company.com) for customers to share their thoughts.
- Listening Forums: Host town hall meetings or Q&A sessions where customers can voice their opinions.

Embed Listening in Company DNA
Encourage listening as a company-wide practice:

- Train employees to actively listen during customer interactions.
- Reward teams that implement customer feedback to improve products or services.

Act on What You Hear
Listening is only valuable if followed by action. When customers see their feedback leading to tangible changes, it fosters loyalty and advocacy.
Building the Listening Infrastructure
Customer Data Systems
Invest in CRM tools that aggregate customer data and provide actionable insights. These systems allow CEOs to have a real-time pulse on customer trends and pain points.
Feedback Analysis
Use AI-powered tools to analyze qualitative feedback from surveys, reviews, and social media. These tools help CEOs identify recurring themes and prioritize areas for improvement.
Listening Squads
Form cross-functional teams dedicated to collecting and analyzing customer insights. These teams can serve as the bridge between customer feedback and executive decision-making.
The Ripple Effect of CEO Listening
When CEOs prioritize customer listening, the impact reverberates throughout the organization:

- Customer-Centric Innovation: Product teams develop solutions that genuinely address customer needs.
- Operational Excellence: Processes are streamlined to remove friction in the customer journey.
- Employee Empowerment: Employees feel motivated to deliver exceptional experiences, knowing that leadership values customer input.

The role of a CEO has evolved from being a top-down decision-maker to becoming a champion of customer voices. By embracing the role of Chief Listener, CEOs like Bhupinder Singh have transformed their organizations into customer-centric powerhouses.

Listening is not just a leadership skill—it's a strategic imperative. CEOs who take the time to engage directly with customers, act on their feedback, and foster a culture of listening set their companies apart in an increasingly competitive market.

CHAPTER IX

Creating a Culture of Customer Obsession

Building a culture of customer obsession isn't just about implementing policies or checking boxes; it's about weaving the customer into the very fabric of your organization. Companies that thrive in competitive markets—whether a QSR giant or a cutting-edge tech firm—understand that prioritizing the customer starts with the workforce. It's about cultivating a mindset where every employee feels personally responsible for delivering value, solving problems, and creating exceptional experiences.

This chapter will explore how to inspire and enable a workforce to prioritize the customer, leadership practices that drive customer-focused excellence, and ways to recognize and reward behaviors that delight customers.

Cultivating a Workforce That Prioritizes the Customer

A customer-obsessed workforce is the foundation of any successful organization. Here's how to cultivate this mindset across your teams:

Make the Customer Real

Often, employees see the customer as an abstract concept. To build empathy and understanding:

- Share Customer Stories: Host regular sessions where customer success stories or pain points are shared. These stories humanize the customer and give employees a tangible sense of impact.
- Bring the Customer In: Invite customers to events, meetings, or feedback panels to share their experiences directly with employees.

Align Roles with Customer Impact

Every role—whether in sales, logistics, or HR—contributes to the customer experience.

- Example: Bhupinder Singh's QSR team conducted a workshop where employees from non-customer-facing departments mapped how their work ultimately impacts the diner's experience. This exercise helped connect everyone's roles to the brand's success.

Provide Training on Customer Empathy
Equip employees with the skills to understand and serve customers better.

- Offer workshops on active listening, empathy-building, and conflict resolution.
- Train teams to anticipate customer needs and proactively address them.

Leadership Practices That Inspire Teams to Go Above and Beyond
Customer obsession begins at the top. Leaders play a critical role in setting the tone and inspiring their teams.

Lead by Example
When leaders visibly prioritize the customer, it sets a powerful precedent.

- Be Present: CEOs and executives should occasionally interact directly with customers. For instance, Bhupinder Singh often visits QSR outlets during peak hours to interact with diners, reinforcing the company's commitment to customer satisfaction.
- Resolve Complaints Personally: Senior leaders can periodically step in to handle customer complaints, demonstrating that no issue is too small for their attention.

Communicate the "Why" Behind Decisions
Help employees understand how every decision supports the customer.

- Example: If introducing a new product feature or policy, explain how it will solve a customer pain point or improve their experience.

Foster Cross-Functional Collaboration
Customer satisfaction often depends on seamless coordination between departments.

- Establish cross-functional teams to address critical customer issues or develop new initiatives.
- Use regular meetings to ensure alignment between marketing, operations, and customer service teams.

Celebrate Successes Publicly
Highlight stories of employees who went beyond for the customer.

- Share these stories in newsletters, town halls, or internal social platforms.
- Use them as teachable moments to inspire others.

Rewarding and Celebrating Customer-Focused Behaviors
Recognition and rewards are essential for reinforcing a culture of customer obsession.

Create Customer-Centric Recognition Programs
Design programs that specifically reward employees for exceptional customer service.

- Monthly Customer Hero Award: Recognize employees who have made a significant impact on customer satisfaction.
- Team-Based Rewards: Celebrate departments or teams that achieve customer-focused goals, such as a reduction in complaints or an improvement in Net Promoter Score (NPS).

Gamify Customer-Focused Metrics
Use gamification to make achieving customer-centric goals engaging and fun.

- Create leaderboards for metrics like response times, positive reviews, or complaint resolutions.
- Offer small incentives for top performers, such as gift cards or extra time off.

Build a Culture of Peer Recognition
Encourage employees to acknowledge each other's customer-focused efforts.

- Set up a peer-to-peer recognition system where employees can nominate colleagues for customer service excellence.
- Use a platform or intranet to share these nominations company-wide.

Tie Customer Metrics to Performance Reviews

Include customer satisfaction metrics (like CSAT or NPS) as part of individual and team performance evaluations.

- For example, make achieving a certain NPS score a key performance indicator (KPI) for frontline teams.

Real-World Examples of Customer-Centric Cultures

The $2,000 Rule

The Ritz-Carlton empowers every employee to spend up to $2,000 to resolve a guest issue without requiring management approval. This policy fosters trust in employees and ensures customer satisfaction is prioritized at every level.

Customer Obsession as a Leadership Principle

Amazon's first leadership principle is "Customer Obsession." Employees are trained to always start with the customer and work backward, which has driven innovations like one-click ordering and same-day delivery.

On-the-Ground Empowerment

In one instance, authorized a team of restaurant managers to design a localized menu item based on customer feedback. The result was a regionally tailored product that became a best-seller, boosting both customer satisfaction and sales.

Breaking Down Barriers to Customer Obsession

Achieving customer obsession often requires overcoming internal challenges.

Eliminate Silos

Departments working in isolation can hinder the customer experience.

- Implement collaborative tools and processes to improve communication across teams.
- Host regular cross-departmental meetings to align on customer goals.

Address Resistance to Change

Not all employees will immediately embrace a customer-first mindset.

- Use training sessions and storytelling to illustrate the benefits of customer obsession.
- Gradually introduce changes and celebrate small wins to build momentum.

Invest in the Right Technology

Provide employees with tools that make it easier to deliver exceptional service.

- Examples include CRM platforms, chatbots for customer service, and real-time analytics dashboards.

The Long-Term Benefits of Customer Obsession

Embedding customer obsession into your company culture yields measurable results:

- Increased Customer Loyalty: Delighted customers are more likely to return and recommend your brand to others.
- Higher Employee Engagement: Employees who see the direct impact of their work on customer satisfaction are more motivated.
- Sustainable Growth: Customer-obsessed companies often enjoy stronger financial performance due to higher retention rates and word-of-mouth marketing.

Creating a culture of customer obsession requires intentionality, effort, and leadership. By cultivating a customer-first mindset, empowering teams, and celebrating customer-focused behaviors, organizations can build a sustainable competitive advantage.

My mentor always says "Happy customers don't just happen; they're the result of a team that listens, learns, and delivers." Let this be the mantra for your organization as you continue your journey toward customer-centric excellence.

CHAPTER X

The ROI of Customer-Centricity

A business that prioritizes customer-centricity isn't just a feel-good endeavor—it's a proven strategy for driving profitability, sustaining growth, and building a lasting competitive edge. In today's dynamic marketplace, customers demand more than just quality products or services. They expect personalized experiences, authentic engagement, and businesses that align with their values. Companies that embrace a "One Customer" approach—where every decision is made with the customer in mind—consistently outperform their competitors.

This chapter explores how focusing on customers drives profitability, fosters brand loyalty, and ensures long-term differentiation in the market.

How Focusing on Customers Drives Profitability and Growth

Customer-centricity goes beyond offering a good product; it's about creating a seamless and memorable experience at every touchpoint. This approach directly influences financial performance in several key ways:

Increased Customer Retention

Retaining an existing customer is significantly more cost-effective than acquiring a new one.

- Statistical Insight: According to Bain & Company, increasing customer retention rates by just 5% can boost profits by 25% to 95%.
- Example: Companies like Amazon invest heavily in convenience and personalization, ensuring customers return for repeat purchases.

Higher Customer Lifetime Value (CLV)

Focusing on the entire customer journey increases CLV, a metric that captures the total revenue a business can expect from a customer over their lifetime.

- Businesses that prioritize customer satisfaction and loyalty enjoy higher CLV, as customers are more likely to make repeat purchases and upgrade to premium offerings.

Positive Word-of-Mouth and Referrals

Delighted customers are your most effective marketers.

- Example: Bhupinder Singh's QSR business experienced a surge in new customers after implementing customer-driven menu innovations. Satisfied diners shared their experiences on social media, driving organic growth without significant marketing spend.

Reduced Customer Acquisition Costs (CAC)
A loyal customer base reduces reliance on expensive marketing campaigns.

- Insight: Satisfied customers often recommend businesses to their friends and family, lowering CAC over time.

Long-Term Benefits of Customer-Centricity
While the immediate financial benefits of customer focus are evident, the long-term advantages ensure sustained success:
Brand Loyalty and Advocacy
Loyal customers not only make repeat purchases but also become vocal advocates for your brand.

- The Emotional Connection: Companies like Apple and Nike have mastered the art of building emotional connections with their customers, ensuring brand loyalty that transcends price wars.
- Metrics: High Net Promoter Scores (NPS) are indicators of strong customer advocacy, leading to increased referrals.

Market Differentiation
In crowded markets, customer experience is often the defining factor that sets brands apart.

- Example: Zappos differentiated itself in the competitive online retail space through unparalleled customer service, offering free shipping, no-hassle returns, and 24/7 support.

Resilience in Market Downturns
Customer-focused companies are better equipped to navigate economic uncertainties.

- Customers are more likely to stick with brands they trust during challenging times, ensuring stable revenue streams.

Key Metrics That Prove the ROI of Customer-Centricity

To quantify the financial impact of customer-centric strategies, businesses must track and analyze the right metrics:

Customer Lifetime Value (CLV)

CLV measures the total revenue generated by a customer over their relationship with your business.

- Formula: A higher CLV indicates strong customer loyalty and effective retention strategies.

Net Promoter Score (NPS)

NPS gauges the likelihood of customers recommending your brand to others.

- Survey Question: "On a scale of 0 to 10, how likely are you to recommend our brand to a friend or colleague?"
- Higher NPS scores correlate with increased word-of-mouth marketing and organic growth.

Churn Rate

The churn rate measures the percentage of customers who stop doing business with you over a given period.

- A low churn rate indicates strong customer retention and satisfaction.

Customer Satisfaction (CSAT)

CSAT surveys assess customers' immediate satisfaction with specific interactions or experiences.

- High CSAT scores reflect successful customer engagement efforts.

First-Contact Resolution (FCR)

FCR measures the percentage of customer issues resolved during the first interaction.

- Improving FCR directly enhances customer satisfaction and reduces operational costs.

Practical Steps to Maximize the ROI of Customer-Centricity
Invest in Customer Insights
Gathering and acting on customer feedback is crucial for staying relevant.

- Use tools like surveys, focus groups, and social listening to understand customer needs and pain points.

Personalize Experiences
Leverage data to deliver personalized experiences that resonate with individual customers.

- Example: Amazon's recommendation engine accounts for 35% of its total sales, highlighting the power of personalization.

Optimize Touchpoints
Every customer interaction is an opportunity to build trust and satisfaction.

- Map the customer journey to identify moments of delight and eliminate friction points.

Continuously Innovate
Use customer feedback as a springboard for innovation.

- Involve customers in co-creation initiatives to ensure new products and services align with their evolving preferences.

Train and Empower Employees
Equip employees with the tools and authority to deliver exceptional customer experiences.

- Empower frontline teams to resolve issues without lengthy approval processes.

The Compounding Benefits of "One Customer" Leadership

The ROI of customer-centricity extends far beyond immediate financial gains. It builds a foundation of trust, loyalty, and advocacy that fuels long-term growth and market leadership. Companies like Amazon, Zappos, and many manufacturing organization have demonstrated that by prioritizing the customer, businesses can achieve sustainable success in even the most competitive industries.

Adopting a customer-first mindset isn't just a strategy—it's a commitment to excellence that touches every corner of an organization. For CEOs and leaders, embracing the "One Customer" approach is not only the key to unlocking financial success but also to creating meaningful, lasting relationships with the people who matter most: your customers.

CHAPTER XI

Overcoming Challenges on the Journey

Embarking on the journey to becoming a "One Customer CEO" is transformative, but it is not without its obstacles. Transitioning an organization to adopt a customer-first approach requires addressing resistance, adapting to shifting expectations, and staying committed even when progress feels slow or uncertain. This chapter delves into the common challenges leaders face on this journey and offers actionable strategies to overcome them, ensuring resilience and momentum.

Common Obstacles to Becoming a *"The One Customer CEO"*

Internal Resistance to Change

- The Challenge: Employees and even leadership teams may resist customer-first initiatives, especially when these changes disrupt established workflows or threaten traditional performance metrics.
- Underlying Cause: Resistance often stems from fear of the unknown, a reluctance to abandon entrenched practices, or skepticism about the ROI of customer-centricity.
- Example: Sales teams accustomed to a quota-driven mindset might resist shifting focus to long-term customer relationships over short-term gains.

Silos Within the Organization

- The Challenge: Many organizations operate in departmental silos where teams focus narrowly on their objectives rather than the broader customer experience.
- Impact: This fragmented approach can lead to inconsistent messaging, disjointed customer journeys, and inefficiencies that erode customer satisfaction.

Misaligned KPIs

- The Challenge: Legacy KPIs may prioritize operational efficiency or profit margins over customer-centric outcomes.

- Impact: Employees may feel torn between delivering exceptional customer experiences and meeting performance metrics that reward speed or cost-cutting.

Evolving Customer Expectations

- The Challenge: Customers' needs and preferences are constantly changing due to market trends, technological advancements, and socio-economic shifts.
- Impact: Keeping up with these changes can be resource-intensive and requires agility in strategy and execution.

Short-Term Financial Pressures

- The Challenge: Investments in customer-centric initiatives often require time before delivering measurable ROI.
- Impact: Leaders may face pressure from stakeholders to prioritize immediate financial returns over long-term customer-focused strategies.

How to Handle Resistance, Both Internally and Externally
Build a Clear Case for Change

- Strategy: Present data and real-world examples that demonstrate the tangible benefits of customer-centricity, such as increased retention, loyalty, and profitability.
- Tip: Highlight success stories from industry leaders like Bhupinder Singh, whose QSR chain thrived by aligning its operations with customer preferences.

Start Small, Then Scale

- Strategy: Launch pilot programs that test customer-first initiatives in specific departments or regions. Use these small wins to build momentum and gather proof points for broader implementation.
- Example: Introduce customer feedback loops in one product line before expanding them company-wide.

Align Incentives Across the Organization

- Strategy: Revise KPIs to reward customer-focused behaviors and outcomes. Ensure every team understands how their role impacts the customer experience.
- Example: Tie bonuses for sales teams to metrics like Net Promoter Score (NPS) rather than just revenue targets.

Empower Cross-Department Collaboration

- Strategy: Break down silos by creating cross-functional teams that work together on customer journey improvements.
- Example: A task force involving marketing, product, and customer support can identify and eliminate pain points in the customer onboarding process.

Address External Resistance Proactively

- Strategy: Communicate transparently with stakeholders who may question the shift to customer-centricity.
- Tip: Provide regular updates on progress, milestones, and the anticipated long-term benefits of the strategy.

Staying Resilient When Customer Expectations Shift

The only constant in customer behavior is change. To maintain a customer-first focus in a dynamic environment, leaders must stay agile and forward-thinking.

Stay Closely Connected to Customers

- Action: Regularly engage with customers through surveys, interviews, and social listening.
- Example: CEOs like Bhupinder Singh frequently visit QSR outlets to observe customer behavior and gather insights firsthand.

Embrace Technology for Real-Time Insights

- Action: Leverage AI-powered analytics tools to track emerging trends, identify shifting preferences, and respond proactively.
- Example: E-commerce platforms use predictive analytics to anticipate customer needs and offer personalized recommendations.

Create an Agile Organizational Framework

- Action: Establish processes that allow teams to pivot quickly in response to changing customer demands.
- Example: Agile methodologies, such as iterative development cycles, can help product teams adapt to customer feedback more efficiently.

Prioritize Transparency During Transitions

- Action: Communicate openly with customers when changes are being made to products, services, or policies.
- Example: Netflix's transparent communication about pricing and subscription model changes helped mitigate customer backlash.

Invest in Continuous Learning and Training

- Action: Regularly upskill employees to ensure they are equipped to meet evolving customer needs.
- Example: Offer workshops on emerging technologies or customer engagement strategies tailored to your industry.

Key Takeaways for Overcoming Challenges

- Understand the Resistance: Identify the root causes of resistance and address them with empathy and data.
- Communicate the Vision: Articulate a clear, compelling case for customer-centricity and how it benefits employees, customers, and stakeholders.
- Be Agile: Stay flexible and open to revising strategies as customer needs evolve.
- Measure Progress: Track metrics like customer satisfaction, NPS, and retention rates to gauge the impact of your efforts.
- Celebrate Wins: Acknowledge and reward teams for their contributions to enhancing the customer experience.

Resilience is the Key to Transformation

The path to becoming a "One Customer CEO" is not linear, nor is it without its challenges. However, overcoming resistance and adapting to change are integral parts of the journey. Leaders who persist, inspire their teams, and stay closely connected to their customers will not only achieve their goals but also set their organizations apart in the marketplace.

The challenges are real, but so are the rewards. By addressing obstacles head-on and staying true to a customer-first vision, you'll cultivate a company culture that thrives on innovation, loyalty, and sustained success.

CHAPTER XII

The Legacy of a "The One Customer CEO"

When a CEO embraces the "One Customer" philosophy, they set in motion a chain of events that reverberates far beyond the company's walls. This legacy is built not just on financial success but on transforming the organization into one that customers love, competitors envy, and stakeholders admire. In this chapter, we'll explore the profound and enduring impact of customer-focused leadership, the inspiration it provides for other leaders, and how it reshapes industries.

Building a Business Customers Love and Competitors Envy

At its core, the legacy of a "The One Customer CEO" lies in building a business that resonates deeply with customers and how this happens:

There is relentless Focus on Value Creation by CEO. When a CEO adopts a customer-first mindset, every decision centers around delivering value.

• Example: Amazon's obsession with customer convenience—evident in innovations like one-click ordering and same-day delivery—has made it the benchmark for customer-centric businesses.

• Outcome: Companies that prioritize customer value foster loyalty, which translates into consistent revenue streams and lower churn rates.

There is Differentiation Through Experience

The customer experience (CX) becomes the ultimate differentiator in competitive markets.

• Example: Apple's focus on creating seamless user experiences across its ecosystem—whether through intuitive design or personalized support—has cultivated a fiercely loyal customer base.

• Outcome: Competitors struggle to match the emotional connection and trust that customer-first companies build.

There is focus on Sustainable Growth Through Advocacy

Satisfied customers don't just return; they bring others along. Word-of-mouth marketing from delighted customers is the most authentic and cost-effective growth driver.

• Example: Tesla's referral program, which rewards loyal customers for bringing in new buyers, has been instrumental in scaling the brand without massive advertising budgets.

The Long-Lasting Impact on the Organization and Market

When a CEO champions customer-centricity, the organization's culture shifts permanently. Employees feel empowered to prioritize customers in their roles, leading to greater job satisfaction and innovation.

• Example: Bhupinder Singh's approach, which instilled a "customer-first" ethos at every level, saw not only higher customer retention but also improved employee morale and performance.

The Industry Leadership plays a role

A "The One Customer CEO" influences not just their company but their entire industry. By setting new standards for service, quality, and innovation, they force competitors to elevate their game.

• Example: Starbucks revolutionized the coffee industry by focusing on customer experience, prompting rivals to rethink their business models and prioritize personalization.

Longevity and Legacy is like path and destination

Customer-focused companies are better equipped to weather market disruptions and economic downturns. Their adaptability and loyalty base ensure resilience.

• Example: Companies like Nike, which constantly evolve by listening to their customers, remain relevant and successful across generations.

Inspiring Other Leaders to Adopt the "One Customer" Philosophy

The influence of a "One Customer CEO" doesn't stop at their organization. Their approach can inspire a broader movement, influencing leaders across industries.

They Lead by Example

CEOs who personally engage with customers demonstrate the importance of direct connection.

• Example: Satya Nadella's empathetic leadership at Microsoft transformed the company's culture, inspiring other tech leaders to prioritize customer understanding.

They Share Success Stories

Sharing the outcomes of customer-centric initiatives, CEOs encourage peers to adopt similar approaches.

• Example: Howard Schultz, former CEO of Starbucks, often spoke about how the company's success was built on understanding and serving its customers.

They Build Networks of Influence

Customer-focused CEOs often collaborate with other leaders, sharing insights and creating industry-wide changes.

• Example: Richard Branson's emphasis on customer experience has inspired countless entrepreneurs to rethink their business strategies.

It's All About the Customer

The "One Customer" mindset is not a passing trend; it's a fundamental shift in how businesses operate. To every CEO reading this, ask yourself:

• Are you truly listening to your customers?

• Are your employees empowered to act in their best interests?

• Is your organization's success tied to customer outcomes?

The answers to these questions will determine whether your company thrives or fades in today's customer-driven marketplace.

The Future of Customer-Centric Businesses

In an era where customers wield more power than ever, businesses that prioritize their needs and expectations will define the future. The companies that lead tomorrow will be those that consistently deliver value, create memorable experiences, and build trust.

Final Reflections

At its heart, customer-centricity is about human connection. It's about understanding, empathy, and the simple yet profound idea of treating customers the way you'd want to be treated. When CEOs embrace this principle, they don't just transform their organizations—they create legacies that inspire and endure.